Chilling
Ghost
Stories

Chilling Ghost Stories

by BERNHARDT J. HURWOOD

Cover by Don Dyen

SCHOLASTIC INC.
New York Toronto London Auckland Sydney

ISBN 0-590-02979-7

12 11 10 9 8 7 6   1 2 3 4 5/9

Printed in the U.S.A.

To Laura

CONTENTS

The House That Didn't Want Anyone to Live in It

It was a bright Saturday morning, and the Holsons were up very early. Everyone was too excited to sleep late because they were moving. Dan and Peggy hadn't seen the "new" house, but their parents had told them it was a big old house perched on a hill.

As soon as they were dressed they ran downstairs for breakfast. Then there was their own last minute packing to do. They wanted to be ready when the moving men came.

When they finally finished, Dan and Peggy had everything packed into three big cartons. And just in time, too! Because the dog began to bark excitedly at the moving van pulling up to the house.

It was several hours drive to the new house, and so it was late afternoon before the movers had everything unloaded and inside. The house *was* big, much bigger than their last house had been. Tall shade trees surrounded it on all sides and made the house quite dark. Peggy and Dan didn't have much time to explore. Their mother was determined to get the beds set up, and clothes, kitchenware and groceries unpacked before dinner.

It was pitch dark outside when the family had finished eating, and they were so tired that their mother suggested they all go to bed. They could finish unpacking, and hang draperies and put down the rugs the next day.

"That's what I call a good idea," said their father. "I'm so tired I could drop." But he wasn't too tired to help make the beds, and in no time at all everyone was ready for bed.

That night Peggy went to sleep in a strange bare room with cartons of books, pictures, and the collection of miniatures still unpacked on the floor. At first she slept very soundly, but then she began dreaming. She dreamed that she was all alone and tied down in a dark room by something she couldn't see or feel. It was an awful feeling. She wanted to cry out, but she couldn't. She just lay there in the dark, helpless and unable to move. And then in her dream the noise began. It wasn't a noise exactly, but a sort of slithery sound — spooky and scary. Suddenly Peggy opened her eyes. She realized that she was no longer dreaming. She was wide awake . . . *but she could still hear the noise!* Hardly breathing, the girl sat up in bed and peered around in the darkness. Something shadowy was moving along the wall! She *hadn't* dreamed it then. It was there in the room with her!

Peggy started screaming, and in a flash, her mother and father and brother came running into the room and turned on the light. The room was bare and empty, but the dog growled softly. Peggy told them what she had seen, and her father said, "Oh come, Peggy, there's nothing in the room. Just look out the window. See the trees? You're just not used to having trees outside your window. You must have heard a branch banging and scraping against the pane. I'm sure that's all it was."

Her mother laughed and added, "You'll

see when I turn out the lights that the trees cast moving shadows in the moonlight. You saw the shadows moving in the room and that frightened you. Just go to sleep. You'll soon get used to the trees and find them comforting."

Dan offered to sit in the room with her until she fell asleep again. But their father said, "It was only a bad dream in a strange room. Peggy will be all right by herself. Won't you, dear?"

Peggy looked doubtful but said, "I guess so." So they kissed her goodnight and left.

But the minute they were gone, Peggy huddled under the blankets and pulled them over her head. Then she began to shake with fright. She was sure she could hear another noise. But she was so tired that she finally dozed off.

The next morning at breakfast everyone joked about Peggy's bad dream. As soon as she was settled in her new room, they said, she wouldn't imagine any slithering sounds or moving things.

That evening, some time after darkness had fallen, something went wrong with the electricity and all the lights went out. "How do you like that?" said their father impatiently. "A fuse must have blown, all of a sudden. I'll have to go down to the cellar and fix it."

"Be sure to take a flashlight," warned mother. "You don't want to trip over anything."

"Don't worry," he promised. "The rest of you just stay where you are till I get back. I don't want *you* tripping over anything, either."

He had barely left the room when the hammering started. It came from upstairs and it sounded as if someone were banging on a pipe with a sledge hammer.

"Good heavens, what's that?" gasped mother.

"Aw, it's probably nothing but a hot water pipe," said Dan. But his voice quavered as if he wasn't so sure.

"I'm scared!" cried Peggy, running over to her mother who put her arms around her.

"Now, Peggy," her mother said, "it's just as Dan says. This is an old house and the pipes may be clogged with rust."

A few minutes later the lights came on and soon afterward Mr. Holson came back upstairs. "Just what I thought," he said.

"A blown fuse. Can't understand how it happened, though. It was brand new . . . and by the way, what were you three up to, anyway? You nearly scared me out of my wits. Now confess, which one of you sneaked down after me and made those squeaking noises on the cellar stairs?"

No one had time to answer, or to tell him about the hammering. Just then the dog came running out of the kitchen, howling, yipping, and crying, his fur bristling. He headed for the sofa and dived underneath. Something had terrified him — but what?

That night nobody slept very well. The dog insisted on staying in Dan's room, and from time to time he would howl, whimper or growl. They heard more banging on the pipes, and doors slammed downstairs.

Monday was a holiday, so Dan and Peggy did not have to go to school and their father stayed home from work. It was a gloomy, rainy day, and breakfast was silent. No one wanted to be the first to talk about the disturbances of the night before. Finally, after breakfast, Peggy said what everyone was beginning to believe. "I don't like this house. I think it's haunted!"

"Now we won't have any of that kind of

talk!" said her father sharply. "Whatever happened last night has to have an explanation. Maybe we don't know what it is now, but we'll find out."

He sounded convincing, but Peggy was sure he didn't really believe what he'd said. A funny look came over her mother's face, and then she smiled and suggested that they go to the movies. "I think we deserve it," she said. "Besides, I think we could all do with some cheering up."

After the movies they still didn't want to go back to the gloomy old house. So, they ate at a Chinese restaurant and had a real feast of about six different dishes of Chinese food.

It was dark when they reached the house. The drizzle had turned to a heavy rain. It slashed against the windowpanes and drummed on the roof. The steady beat had a soothing, reassuring sound to Peggy when she went to bed, and she soon fell fast asleep. How long she slept she couldn't have said, but suddenly she was caught in the same nightmare that had terrified her so on the first night. Again, she was all alone, tied down in the dark, empty room, unable to move, unable to scream — and once again she heard the fearful, soft, slithering sound.

Still in the dream, Peggy took a deep breath, determined to scream as loud as she could. She woke up with a start, and discovered she *was* screaming — so loud that she must have been awakened by the sound of her own voice. Though the room was almost pitch dark, a faint light came from the window, and over in one corner Peggy could see something like a huge dark figure moving slowly.

Just then everyone came running into the room. Peggy was so frightened she couldn't talk, but when her mother turned on the light she found her voice and half sobbing, told what had happened.

"Now Peggy," said her father, shaking his head, and pointing to the corner of the room. "Don't you remember, I put your mother's dress form there yesterday. Look!" He went over to the corner, lifted the cape that covered it, and stood aside. "See," he added. "Nothing but the dress form."

After the lights had gone out again and everyone had returned to their rooms, Dan came tiptoeing back to Peggy's bedside. "Shhh," he whispered. "You go to sleep, sis, and I'll sit in the chair until you go to sleep. Okay?"

"Oh, thanks Dan," she said with a sigh. "I feel better now. I'll go to sleep, honest I will."

"Don't worry, then. Just go to sleep."

"All right."

But after five minutes or so, she called out, "Dan . . . ?"

"Aren't you asleep yet?"

"Do you believe me. . . . I mean, do you really believe I saw something move?"

"Gee, I don't know. . . . Maybe it was some kind of a shadow from the trees outside. Who knows? Now c'mon, please, go to sleep."

Peggy was beginning to get sleepy now, and so was Dan. They both dozed, Peggy huddled under the covers in bed, and Dan in the chair. All of a sudden the window began rattling and the floorboards started to squeak. Peggy sat bolt upright in bed and Dan gripped the arms of the chair. He was just about to jump up and turn on the lights when a terrible, cackling laugh filled the air. It came from the corner, and as their eyes grew accustomed to the dark they could see instead of the dress form, a laughing skeleton with a flapping black cape. . . . it glowed a horrible greenish color and it seemed to float toward them.

This time they both began screaming. Their mother and father burst into the room, and everyone began talking at once. When Peggy told what she had seen she had Dan to back up her story. And this time their parents believed Peggy's experiences had been real.

The next morning Dan and Peggy went to their new school. When the other children found out that they had just moved into the house on the hill, they grew wide-eyed. No one ever lived there for long, they said, because the house was haunted.

That evening Dan and Peggy told their mother and father what they had heard at school, and then their parents did some investigating of their own. As a result, before the week was over, they were packing to move from The House That Didn't Want Anyone to Live in It.

What the Gravedigger Saw

MANY YEARS AGO, a grave digger named
Murdoch lived in a lonely, windswept moun-
tain village.

As it was only a tiny hamlet, the grave
digger did not have work to do every day
and sometimes went to neighboring villages
to dig graves when it became necessary. And
on those days when Murdoch was happy
working, others were sad because of a death.
It seemed that when Murdoch smiled, others
wept. Only during such mournful times did
he earn his daily bread.

On this day, he was especially happy
about his work. The grave he had to dig was

for a woman who had caused nothing but trouble for everyone around her. She had been mean and cruel all of her life. Not only people, but animals too, had suffered because of her cruelties. And it seemed to Murdoch not even the smallest, most helpless kitten had been safe from her cruel hands — and he couldn't forget that.

So to make sure that she stayed in her grave, he decided to dig it extra deep. Before starting his work, he carefully placed a package on a nearby grave. "I mustn't forget this," he said to himself. "If I do, my wife will be furious." And he set to work.

When he was finished, he left the cemetery to perform a similar job in a neighboring town twenty miles away. It was late afternoon before he started on the long trip back to his own village. The shadows grew long and the chill night winds began to blow. He was almost home when he remembered the package that he had left in the cemetery early in the morning. Angry at himself for not having remembered to take it with him when he left, he made his way back to the little graveyard.

It was dark and the moon was hidden by clouds when Murdoch finally reached the cemetery gates. It was now nearly midnight and he was as tired as he was annoyed. Being accustomed to cemeteries and graves he wasn't afraid of anything but the tongue-lashing he knew his wife would give him when he arrived home so late.

Pushing the creaky iron gate open he hurried through and made his way between the rows of tombstones and mounds. Luckily he remembered exactly where he had left the package and sure enough, there it was, undisturbed and waiting for him to retrieve it. He had barely picked it up when he heard the crunch of carriage wheels on the gravel road and the pounding of horses' hoofs. Murdoch whirled to face the road. "Who would be coming here at this hour?" he wondered, fearfully. Louder and louder grew the sounds as the mysterious vehicle came closer.

Then in the darkness he made out the shape that approached. It was a hearse — or at least a carriage that looked very much like one. Though Murdoch was not a timid man, a sudden chill went down his spine and he ducked behind a tree. And just in time! Rumbling around the bend as though pursued by the devil himself the carriage roared straight through the cemetery gates! The horses were jet black steeds with terrible glowing red eyes. Their manes flew about their heads and blue sparks flew when their hoofs smote the ground as they came to a halt. They stood there snorting and stomping and foaming at the mouth, and the doors of the carriage flew open. Murdoch could see two dark figures climb out, but all he could see of their faces were terrible greenish-yellow eyes.

Terrified now beyond all measure, he dropped to the ground and peered through a clump of grass, watching in horror as they stalked noiselessly straight toward him — and to the very grave he had dug that morning. Then they seemed to dip down and disappear into the earth.

From his hiding place Murdoch thought he could hear a scraping sound. Then suddenly he heard the most unearthly scream of his life. It made the blood run cold in his veins. It went on and on and on rising and falling like the wind, echoing through the night like a thousand demons, or a thousand souls in agony.

Frozen with fear he crouched there expecting his own end to come at any moment, then the two dark figures reappeared — this time with a third figure robed in white, struggling and writhing in their grip. Desperately it tried to break away. Sobbing, wailing, moaning, and crying, the wretched figure tried to break loose from its captors. In a flash the three were down the path and alongside the hearse. There the white-robed figure screamed again and wrenched loose for an instant.

In that second the moon rolled from behind the clouds — and Murdoch's heart stood still! There, standing by the dark hearse was the cruel woman whose grave Murdoch had dug only that morning. And holding her in their claws, *were two giant black cats!*

The Pirate Ghost of Gombi Isle

IN THE BAYOU COUNTRY of Louisiana they tell all sorts of weird tales about ghosts and spirits and werewolves and devils. They say that Gombi Island, just beyond the mouth of Caillou Bayou, is haunted by the ghost of a ferocious pirate who skulks about after dark to protect his buried treasure.

Once a young man named Louis decided he wasn't going to be put off by any ghosts, and made up his mind to go to Gombi Island at night and dig up the treasure for himself. Nighttime would be best, for he feared the daylight hours even more, when the tough waterfront hoodlums would steal the treasure from him if they knew he had found it.

So one night he slipped from his house, went down to the bayou where he kept a small boat, and started rowing toward the island. It didn't take him long to get there, and when he did he beached the canoe, took out his shovel, selected a likely spot near an old tree, and began to dig. Suddenly he heard a suspicious noise. Whirling around he saw that his canoe was slipping into the water all by itself. Splashing in after it he managed to grab it and drag it back, this time taking it well up on the shore where he tied it to a tree for good measure. With that he went back to his digging.

He had barely dug two or three feet down when he heard another sound, this time behind him . . . right behind him! Somebody was there. He could tell. Scared nearly out of his wits he looked over his shoulder. He almost died on the spot. There glaring at him were three pirates with long black beards, pistols in their belts, cutlasses at their waists, and long gleaming daggers in their hands. Blood dripping from the knives, water dripped down from their clothes, and seaweed was tangled in their beards and hair.

Convinced that he was done for, poor

Louis shut his eyes tight and began to pray. After a minute or two, as nothing had happened to him, he opened one eye and peered up. The pirates had vanished. But so had Louis' courage. Now he wasn't interested in the gold anymore, only in getting back to his canoe and home to bed.

Scrambling from the hole he had dug and clutching his shovel, he ran to the boat as fast as he could. But suddenly he stopped in his tracks. There sitting in the boat was still another pirate. He was bigger than the others and he wore a long coat with a big shiny belt, a black cocked hat, huge gleaming golden earrings, and heavy, muddy boots. His beard was longer and blacker than the other three, and he was more terrifying to look at, too. Like the others he appeared to be soaking wet. Blood dripped down his face, and, tangled in his moustache and beard, were squirming live shrimps and slimy strands of seaweed.

Seizing a pistol from his belt with a great hairy paw of a hand the pirate rose up and snarled in a hollow voice, "Get in and row, ye miserable lubber!"

Shaking like a leaf Louis did as he was told, rowing as if the devil himself was after him. As soon as they were half way between the island and the shore, the pirate stood up in the boat, put his pistol back in his belt, threw back his head and laughed hideously. Then springing over the side he sank to the bottom of the bayou . . . blub! Just like that. Louis watched as he disappeared beneath the water, like a corpse with an anchor around its ankles, disappearing without a trace, without even a bubble.

When he got home and burst through the front door of his house poor Louis' wife let out a bloodcurdling scream and rushed to her room bolting the door behind her.

It wasn't until Louis glimpsed himself in the mirror that he understood why. She hadn't recognized him. He hardly recognized himself. And no wonder! *His hair had turned snow white!*

The Midnight Ghost

MARY DRAKE lived and taught school in a small English village. One Christmas she received an invitation to go to London to spend the holidays with a distant cousin who lived in a great mansion that was hundreds of years old. She was very excited, because not only was her cousin very rich, but he was an earl, and she knew that she would have a very elegant time.

Mary had not seen her cousin since she was a little girl, so she was disappointed when he did not meet her on her arrival. His wife, Lady Margaret was very proper, but certainly not friendly. Mary was doubly disappointed when a butler showed her to the room in which she was to dine when she arrived — a large gloomy ballroom. What made matters worse, she was to eat all by herself. She had gotten there too late for dinner, and for reasons she did not understand, all the other guests and members of the household were otherwise occupied.

The ballroom was dimly lighted and very lonely. When she finished eating, Mary was about to leave and go to bed, when the butler came in and asked her if she would mind waiting there for a while until her room was made ready. Feeling as though there was some mysterious reason why they did not want to let her go anywhere else, she sat in a chair by the huge fireplace and began to wish that she had never come. The fire soon died down and the room began to grow chilly. Shivering slightly, she began to think back to her childhood days. She remembered the good times she used to have. Her thoughts were interrupted by a cold blast of air down the chimney. The fire flickered and grew dim. Mary shivered again and drew her shawl around her shoulders. The room seemed to have grown darker and the far corners seemed to be enveloped in shadows impossible to penetrate.

Now as she looked around she became aware of moonlight shining through the elegant diamond-shaped windowpanes making a silvery trail across the rich oriental carpet. Glancing from one magnificent piece of furniture to another, Mary began to imagine what it must have been like in the days when the room was filled with handsome men and beautiful women, all wearing velvets and brocades and laces and silks. She could visualize the golden glow of candlelight, bathing the room in a warm glow, and she could almost hear the murmur of voices, the tinkle of glasses, and the sound of music from an earlier time.

Suddenly her pleasant thoughts vanished. An icy chill came over her and once again she was aware of the darkness and gloom. But there was something else she felt. Something terrifying. Something incredibly evil. She couldn't see anything. She couldn't hear anything. But she could feel a crawling sensation all over. She wanted to scream, but her voice was frozen in her throat. She wanted to rise from her chair and run away, but she was paralyzed with terror.

There, before her eyes, on a small patch of the carpet something was moving. Fixing her gaze on it she saw at once that it was rising through the floor. First just a shapeless black blob . . . then, Heaven help her! . . . a hideous head with long matted black hair hanging down on either side. It was the face of something dreadful. Slowly it kept rising, up . . . up . . . it was more than a head now but a whole body, a figure of something that had once been human, but now, ravaged by decay and time it was ugly and awful. Tattered rags hung down in shreds from its bony limbs, and in its arms was clutched a pitiful and withered figure that might have been a child.

Facing Mary briefly, its empty eye sockets staring without seeing, the apparition turned and glided noiselessly across the room and disappeared in the shadows. The moment it vanished she felt a strange calmness come over her and she began to suspect that perhaps there was a reason for her having been left alone in this room. But she had no more opportunity to think about the matter because just then her cousin Roger entered, and greeted her so warmly that she nearly forgot the terrible phantom she had seen.

The next morning at breakfast Lady Margaret asked Mary if she had been disturbed by anything the night before. Mary could tell at once that her hostess was afraid of something, but was not going to reveal what it was. So she only said she had enjoyed a very quiet evening, and then they fell to talking of other things.

That evening after dinner Mary was once again asked to wait in the ballroom until her bed was made up for her. As she sat there clutching the arms of her chair, the hideous ghost arose again from the depths beneath the ballroom floor. Just as on the previous night, it hovered, clasping its pitiful burden in its gaunt arms, then slowly turned to drift across the chilly room and disappear from sight in the gloom.

Breakfast the next morning was exactly as it had been on the first day. Lady Margaret appeared nervous, and questioned Mary. How did she sleep? Did anything at all bother her or frighten her during the night? And as before, Mary only smiled and said that everything had been lovely.

For three more nights Mary was forced to endure the sight of the dreadful specter that arose from beneath the ballroom floor.

And for three more mornings she had to undergo the same sort of questioning by Lady Margaret. But after breakfast on the fourth morning, Mary detected something different in her hostess's manner — she seemed to be not at all nervous.

"Roger," she said to her husband. "Today we must have the ballroom floor polished and get everything ready for the ball."

The next three days were spent in feverish preparation for the annual New Year's Eve Ball, but with a difference, Mary found out. For the first time in the memory of anyone in the house the ballroom was going to be used for the occasion. The old butler confided to her that it had always been kept shut, and that the master of the house had been the only one ever to enter it.

Strange! Mary thought. Even Lady Margaret had never set foot in the room before. Very strange indeed!

The ball was everything that Mary had hoped it would be. There were rainbow colored decorations of every description. Banners, streamers, flowers, and balloons. The floor was gleaming and spotless. All the heavy, dark, gloomy furniture was gone, and in its place, bright cheerful chairs and tables — the latter laden with crystal decanters, sparkling silver, and gleaming china platters heaped with delicacies.

Despite the changes that had been made, despite the brilliant light, the laughing guests, and the cheerful music, Mary sensed a peculiar feeling of foreboding. But with the arrival of more guests, with the dancing, and the celebrating, she soon forgot her fears. Then about five minutes before midnight she noticed her cousin glancing nervously at his watch, and then stare at the precise spot before the fireplace from which the terrible apparition had appeared every night.

Suddenly someone cried out, "Happy New Year!" The musicians struck up the strains of *Auld Lang Syne,* and everyone began singing and calling "Happy New Year!" Only two people in the room refrained from the gaiety — Mary and her cousin, Roger. A quick look passed between them, and before either could say a word a terrible head began rising up from beneath the floor. Words froze on people's lips. The musicians stopped playing. Laughter turned to screaming as the hideous apparition rose to its full height, glided up to Lord Roger, bared its teeth in an unspeakably fearsome grimace, and shook its fist in his face, while clutching its loathsome burden with the other hand.

As guests, servants and musicians fled screaming from the ballroom, Mary saw the color drain from her cousin's face, and Lady Margaret moaned and slumped to the floor in a faint.

The next day Roger, looking drawn and pale, told Mary the story of the phantom of the ballroom. Centuries ago an ancestor had murdered a young woman and her infant, then buried them beneath the ballroom floor. Conscience stricken, he died soon after, but before breathing his last he commanded that the ballroom never again be used for a joyous purpose, otherwise disaster would strike. "The reason we placed you in that room every night," Roger confessed shamefacedly, "was that every December from the 20th to the 31st the apparition was said to appear at midnight — but only to a member of the family. I never saw it, but we decided to see what happened if *you* were left alone there. Then, when you said nothing about what you had seen afterward, we assumed the story was nothing but rubbish, and we made up our minds to have the ball."

"I'm sorry," said Mary. "If I had known the story I would have told you everything."

"It's too late now, I'm afraid," sighed Roger. "You must leave at once. I can't permit you to share in our punishment — whatever it may be."

Mary left that day — and none too soon! That very night a mysterious fire burned the great mansion to the ground!

The Haunted Clock

THERE WAS ONCE a miserly old farmer who lived in an isolated part of the country, far from the nearest city. His farm had none of the modern conveniences such as telephones, electricity, or hot and cold running water. He was mean to his family and to his hired hands alike, so when he died no one was particularly sorry to see him go.

Everyone thought that because he had been such a skinflint his widow and son would be very well off, but that wasn't the case at all. There was no money left to them and there was as much work as ever to be done — and one pair of hands less to help with it.

The old man had barely been laid in the ground when strange noises began to be heard in the house after dark. Mysterious footsteps trudged up and down the hallways. Doors opened and closed by themselves, the floorboards squeaked, and windows rattled and shook. On moonless nights the wind howled and shook the rafters. When there was no wind, frightening moans and wails echoed through the house. And dark shadows could sometimes be seen slipping around corners of rooms where no proper shadows had any right to be seen.

On the first Christmas after the farmer's death, a hired hand named Joe promised to sit up and wait for the mistress of the farm and her son to come home. They had gone to spend Christmas Eve with some neighbors and were not planning to return until very late.

It was cold and dark, so to keep warm and comfortable, Joe sat in the kitchen, which was very old fashioned and cozy. It had a huge fireplace on one side, a coal-burning stove on the other, and on one wall a big china closet filled with all sorts of dishes. Near the china closet, facing the door to the next room, stood a tall old grandfather clock. It rested firmly in a special niche in the floor that had been made by removing several of the tiles, and its loud ticking kept Joe company as he sat before the blazing fire and read by the light of a single candle.

As it grew late the fire settled down to a warm glow, and the candle burned down to a nub and flickered out. Joe was too tired to light another candle and continue reading, so he settled comfortably back in his chair to snooze a while. He was just beginning to doze off when he heard the outer door open. Thinking it was the widow and her son coming home, he got up and prepared to go to greet them. Suddenly he saw an old man with a long white beard come through the door and cross the room to the clock, where he stood and stared. It was too dark to see the old man's face, so he ran over and called out, "Stop! Who are you?"

The old man turned around and Joe gasped. It couldn't be, yet there was no mistaking him. It was the old farmer . . . or his ghost!

As Joe stood there gaping, the old man walked back through the door in the direction from which he had come. Joe bounded after him and grabbed the doorknob to prevent the ghost from closing the door. And at that moment something strange happened to him. His hand stuck to the knob as if it were glued to it. No matter how hard he tried to pull it free it stayed in place, and at the same time he felt a terrible chill come over him as though he had been suddenly swallowed up in a cake of ice. He tried turning the knob to the right and to the left, but it wouldn't budge. He was terrified, but he couldn't move his feet either. All he could do was stand there and shiver. Finally he was freed from the grip of whatever it was that had been holding him and he ran to the next room. It was empty.

The next day Joe packed his bag and told the widow he was quitting. "I'm not spending another night in this house," he said. "It's haunted." Then he told her all about what had happened, explaining that it wasn't the sight of the old man's ghost that had scared him so, but having been stuck to the doorknob afterward when he had grabbed it.

The woman had no reason to doubt Joe's word, because he had always been a very honest man, besides, she had suspected for quite some time that the house was haunted.

The only reason she had never said anything about it was that she hadn't wanted to frighten anyone else.

"There's only one thing for us to do," she said. "We have to look in the clock."

They opened the clock and looked in every nook and corner, but could find nothing out of the ordinary. Just wheels and springs and dust.

"I know the ghost was trying to tell us something," she insisted. "I guess we'll have to look underneath the clock."

So she and Joe and her son struggled to move the huge grandfather clock away from where it stood. It was a very difficult job because it was so heavy. But once they finished moving it their efforts were rewarded. There, directly under the floor where the clock had stood was a sturdy wooden chest with iron bands.

When they opened it they found a hoard of money — more than enough to modernize the farm and live comfortably from that time on. Joe was handsomely rewarded, so he didn't quit after all, and the ghost of the farmer never returned again.

A-Ling and the Evil Spirits

Long ago in the Chinese city of Soochow there lived a young man named A-Ling who worked in the household of a rich scholar named Han.

One night after bringing a pot of tea to a guest who was staying in the house of Han, A-Ling said, "Downstairs, just now I met a fierce-looking stranger in white. He did not answer me when I challenged him. I think he may be an evil spirit."

The guest made fun of A-Ling who became embarrassed and left. The next night as the guest came downstairs, he stumbled over a body on the ground floor. It was

A-Ling. There were bruise marks on his neck and face, but he was alive and breathing.

When he was able to talk he said, "I saw the stranger in white again. Tonight he had a short white beard and his face looked as though fire had blackened it. As he seized my throat and began to strangle me, another spirit appeared. This one had a long white beard and a tall cap. He said, 'Spare him, he is too young to die!' But the one who was choking me would not listen. Just then they must have seen you. They immediately disappeared — but I *know* they are still in this house!"

A-Ling was then put to bed and several persons sat up with him. All night long strange and mysterious lights that looked like fireflies flitted to and fro about the room. In the morning A-Ling behaved strangely and refused to eat. Seeing this his master, Han, sent for a magician to examine the ailing young man. The magician declared, "He is possessed by an evil spirit. Bring me a writing brush and vermilion ink, and I will tell you what spells to write with it."

The brush and ink were brought and the magician said, "Over his heart brush on the character meaning 'Uprightness.' Upon his neck, the character for 'sword,' and upon each of his hands, the character, 'fire.' Thus will you cure him."

Han did as he was told. Just as he was brushing on the character 'fire' for the second time, the evil spirit shrieked, "Do not burn me! Let me depart!" And in a twinkling the evil spirit left A-Ling's body, fleeing from the house, never to return. And no one in Han's household was ever bothered again.

The Magician

Many many years ago a beautiful red haired lady whose name was Isobel married a captain in the British Indian Army. They went to live in a hot, dusty, little East Indian village at the edge of a dark and mysterious jungle where he was stationed.

Mrs. Oak had never been to India before, and she was enchanted by the sights and sounds and smells of the country. After arriving in Calcutta by ship they had to travel by horse drawn carriage to their final destination. The journey was dangerous, for in those times the mountains and the jungles and the open countrysides were infested with bandits.

Naturally Captain and Mrs. Oak were very relieved when they finally reached the village. As the captain had lived there before getting married, he already had a fine bungalow on the outskirts of town near the edge of the jungle. When they came to the bungalow, Mrs. Oak noticed a ragged, dirty, evil-looking man squatting on the ground near the front door. There was something about the way his eyes gleamed that made her shudder.

Inside the bungalow she asked her husband about the man, but Captain Oak said, "Oh, don't worry about him. He's been here as long as I have. No one pays any attention to him."

"But he frightens me," she said. "I don't like his looks. Won't you please send him away?"

"One doesn't do things like that here, my dear," replied the captain smiling. "We might insult him, and it wouldn't do at all to offend a native of this place . . . especially him."

"What's so special about him?" she asked.

Her husband laughed. "The villagers consider him a very important man. They say he's a powerful magician, and they're all frightfully afraid of him. Naturally, I don't believe in these things."

So that was that. Nevertheless, every day, when the old man came and sat down near the front door of the bungalow poor Mrs. Oak felt uncomfortable. But she knew that it would do no good to say anything. She tried to avoid looking at the old man, but he drew her attention the way a magnet attracts iron. There he would sit, staring at her with those dark, glowing eyes, and try as she might she could not keep from staring back into them. She felt like a bird being drawn into the clutches of a stalking cat.

Several days after arriving at the bungalow her husband was called away on duty and Mrs. Oak was left alone. Her first night was terrifying. Strange, unearthly wails seemed to float from the jungle. She had the feeling that there were creepy crawly Things trying to slip through her bedroom window, and even after she finally drifted off to sleep she had nightmares in which the old man with the dirty matted beard and piercing eyes chased her in a dark brambly wood. As he bore down on her roaring like a wild beast, the branches of the trees reached out to her like bony claws clutching, scratching, grabbing. . . .

As the days passed Mrs. Oak felt worse and worse. The heat grew unbearable, her head ached and throbbed, and her nerves felt as though they would never stand such strain. One day, while Captain Oak was still away, she went out for a breath of air, and sat on the verandah to read a book. But as she sat there she felt the skin begin to crawl at the back of her neck. It was as if someone were staring at her and about to spring. Whirling around she saw at once that the cause of her discomfort was the old man with the beard. He was glaring at her with a terrible gleam in his eyes, and she was so upset that she finally stood up, pointed her finger at him, and cried, "You there, go away, you frighten me!"

Instead of answering her he just sat there still as a statue looking neither to the right nor to the left, but fixing her with that frightening glare. Mustering up all the courage she could, Mrs. Oak again ordered him to go away. For a moment he just sat there as he had before, but then he said very slowly, "Only if you give me a hair from your head."

"A *hair!*" she exclaimed, trying to hide her fear. "Oh, very well. I suppose I can cut one. Wait here. I'll be back."

Now when the old man had spoken to her she had been so frightened she had felt unable to move. Then the moment she promised to give him what he wanted it was as though a strange power had been lifted and she could go.

Rushing into the house she went to her bedroom and took out her scissors. She was terribly worried. She had heard all sorts of stories about Indian sorcerers and she knew that somehow this frightening old man must be one of them, and that he had wanted the strand of hair for some unspeakable and evil reason. "I mustn't give him one hair of my head," she thought. "If I do, something dreadful will happen! I'm sure of it. But I *must* give him something. Oh, dear, what shall I do?"

As she stood there wondering and worrying her eyes fell on a Chinese red mat woven of hair. "That's what I'll do," she thought. "I'll give him a hair from the mat."

It was easy enough to pull a long hair

from the red mat. She hurried back to the front steps and sighing in relief, gave it to him. The old man took it and walked away.

That night when Captain Oak came home, his wife told him what had happened. He was annoyed at first, because she had spoken to the old man. But seeing how happy she was at having gotten rid of the unwelcome visitor so easily, the matter was soon forgotten and they talked of other things.

About a week later something very strange happened. Mrs. Oak, who had been feeling rather ill all day, suddenly rose from the dinner table before finishing her coffee. She raised her hands before her and began staggering toward the window. Moaning as she walked, she looked exactly like a sleepwalker or person in a trance. Then, swaying slightly, she cried out once and collapsed to the floor in a faint.

Running to her in alarm Captain Oak lifted her in his arms. But just as he started to carry her toward the shadowy hallway, he suddenly heard a strange sound coming from that direction. It was a muffled flapping. He stopped and listened. Flap . . . flap . . . flap. And in between the flaps was a soft sliding dragging sound, becoming louder and louder as it grew closer.

Hastily putting his unconscious wife on the sofa, Captain Oak rushed to the closet and took out his service revolver. He bounded toward the hallway then stopped in the darkness and listened. Flap. Flap. Flap. Closer and closer it came. Straining to see, he was suddenly seized by a kind of paralysis. No matter how hard he tried he couldn't move a muscle. Flap . . . flap . . . flap. The dreadful sound went right past him and toward the verandah. Worst of all he could not see what it was.

Then, as quickly as the paralyzed feeling had come over him it left. Pistol in hand he rushed to the door. Now the flapping noise could be heard on the verandah outside. Dashing out to settle the matter once and for all, Captain Oak peered through the darkness and thought he could see a dark shape slithering toward the steps. Waiting no longer he raised the revolver and fired three times.

The sound of the gunfire aroused his wife who ran to his side. They were joined moments later by the servants, who gathered around chattering nervously. Then arming themselves with lanterns and clubs they all began to search, fully prepared to find the bullet riddled body of an intruder.

Mrs. Oak suddenly cried out, "Look! Over there!"

Rushing to where she pointed they all froze in their tracks. There on the steps leading down from the verandah lay the Chinese mat from the bedroom — and in the middle of it were *three fresh bullet holes!*

The Thing

At the outskirts of a faraway city there was a lonely road that curved and twisted around a bare and rocky hill. There were no lights for miles around and those who had to walk there after dark always carried lanterns. Then it became known that the road began to be haunted by a Thing — a Thing so frightening that no one who saw it could ever describe it.

Very late one night an old man was hurrying along that lonesome stretch of road, wishing that he were somewhere else instead, when he saw a woman sitting on a stone and crying bitterly. Seeing that she was so troubled, he stopped to offer her any help that he could.

"My dear lady," he said. "Please do not cry like that. Tell me what your trouble is, and if there is any way in which I can help you I shall be glad to do so."

But instead of answering she wept all the harder, hiding her face in the sleeves of her coat. "Please, dear lady," he said again, as gently as he could. "Listen to me. This is no place for a woman alone at night. Tell me, how can I help you?" Slowly she rose up, but turned her back to him, moaning and sobbing as she moved. So he put his hand lightly on her shoulder and said, "Listen to me, please, just for a moment . . ."

Then the sobbing woman turned to him slowly . . . slowly, and dropped her arm from before her face. And the man saw that she had no eyes or nose or mouth or ears. Her face was smooth and blank as an egg! He screamed and ran as fast as he could.

Up the lonely road he went. All was darkness and emptiness. On and on he ran as fast as his old legs would carry him, never daring to look back. At last he saw a lantern ahead. It was so far away that it looked like the glow of a firefly, and he hurried toward it. It proved to be the lantern of a sausage vendor, who had set up a stand alongside the lonely road. The old man was so happy to see another human being after his terrifying experience that he didn't even wonder why a sausage vendor would be on this lonely, untraveled road at night. He flung himself at the sausage vendor's feet, panting and crying, "Aah! . . . Aah! . . . Aah! . . ."

"Here! Here!" exclaimed the sausage man gruffly. "What's the matter with you? Did anyone hurt you?"

"Nobody hurt me," gasped the other . . . "Only . . . Aah! . . . Aah! . . ."

"Oh, they only scared you," declared the peddler. "Were they robbers?"

"N-no, not robbers," stammered the terrified man. "I saw . . . I saw a woman . . . on . . . on a rock . . . and she showed me . . . Aah! . . . I can't tell you what she showed me! . . ."

"Ha! Was it anything like *this* that she showed you?" cried the sausage man. He lifted his hand to his face, and turned toward the flickering lantern light the old man carried.

Horror-struck, the old man saw no eyes, no nose, no mouth, but a face — *smooth and bare as an egg.*

And in that dreadful moment, the flickering lanterns went out, leaving the old man in the darkness *with the Thing.*

The Woman in Green Velvet

DARK AND GLOOMY CLOUDS were gathering
ominously in the gray November sky, but
Lucy Carter hummed cheerfully to herself
as she drove along the deserted Massachu-
setts highway. The Thanksgiving holiday
had just begun, and she had a week off from
her studies at the University.

Lucy was looking forward to Thanksgiving, more this year than ever, because it
would also be a family reunion at the home
of her Aunt Dorcas and Uncle Seth. They
lived in a rambling old house on Cape Cod
not far from Provincetown. Tomorrow there
would be turkey with all the trimmings,

homemade mince and pumpkin pies, and all the other delicious things that Aunt Dorcas would prepare for the Thanksgiving feast — and right here on Cape Cod where the holiday first began.

Provincetown was still a good three hours drive ahead, when there was an ear-splitting thunderclap, and the sky grew so dark that Lucy had to turn on the headlights. A jagged streak of lightning flashed across the horizon and she realized that any minute the rain would come pouring down. Then came a second clap of thunder that rumbled with such force the little car seemed to tremble. Lucy felt a tiny thrill of panic, even though she knew there was nothing to fear. But the thought of being alone on the road, buffeted about by the rising storm winds from off the sea, made her wish she were already in Aunt Dorcas's friendly kitchen.

"Who'd have thought there'd be a thunderstorm in November!" she exclaimed aloud as the rain came down in sheets, lashed by the wind. It was all but impossible to see the road ahead, and it was rapidly becoming too dangerous to drive. She slowed the car to a crawl then turned on the radio for company. It was no use. Static drowned out everything. "If I saw a place to stop, I would," Lucy said to herself. "At this rate I won't get there until midnight."

Lucy wasn't accustomed to driving at night, but as there seemed to be no letup in the storm, she decided she must. And finding a place to spend the night wouldn't be easy. Most places on the Cape where people found lodgings for the night, were open only in the summer, and here it was — near the end of November. If only she could see the light of even a tourist home! She gripped the steering wheel tighter as she drove, and as the storm grew worse time seemed to stand still. Creeping along at a snail's pace, Lucy watched the sky gradually darken into black night.

Then in the blurred glow of the headlights Lucy saw a sign — INN. She slowed the car to a stop, and in a flash of lightning read the faded, peeling letters — OLD GRAYSTONE INN TURN RIGHT 3 MILES.

Would it be open this time of the year? Lucy hoped so. Taking heart she put the car in forward gear again and began watching for the turn-off to the inn.

When she reached it, she found it was a narrow, muddy, bumpy lane. She drove along anxiously, looking for a glimpse of the inn. But all was pitch black. Lucy began to worry.

But then, about a thousand feet ahead, a faint light shone through the driving rain.

A few minutes later Lucy was alongside Old Graystone Inn. A gloomy old-fashioned building, it appeared dark and uninviting. Had it not been for a few dim beams of light escaping through the cracks of the shuttered windows on the ground floor it might well have appeared deserted. She had small hopes of being able to get a room, for a large sign on the front door read CLOSED. But having come this far, Lucy determined to try. The worst that could happen was that she might be turned away.

Shutting off the ignition and headlights, Lucy pulled up her coat collar, and reached for her overnight bag. She hurried out of the car, and ran through the driving rain to the front door of the inn. There was a huge brass knocker, now green with age and exposure. She knocked several times, shivering in the cold wind from the sea. Finally she heard shuffling footsteps inside, and a few moments later the door creaked open. A dried-up old man appeared. He had skin like parchment and dull bloodshot eyes.

"We're closed. What d'ye want?" he croaked in a raspy, unpleasant voice.

"Please," said Lucy. "It's late and this

storm is terrible. Couldn't I have a room for the night? I'd even sleep in the lobby on a sofa — anything to get out of this storm!"

"Let her in, Caleb," came a voice from the darkness beyond, a woman's voice. "T'isn't a fit night fer anyone to be out be they quick or be they dead."

It was a strange hollow voice that somehow made Lucy shudder, yet, she was glad of the opportunity to get in out of the storm. The old man stepped aside and closed the door. The old fashioned kerosene lamp he carried threw long, flickering shadows. He muttered, "Ye'd be better off if'n ye didn't stay, but ye can have room 13 there — t'end of the passage." He stopped, raised his lamp, and pointed a long bony finger to the last room at the end of a long corridor.

"How much will that be for the night?" asked Lucy.

"I don't aim t'bargain with ye, miss. Take it or leave it!"

"Oh, I'll take it," she answered quickly. But already she was beginning to wish that she had not stopped at all. Without another word, the old man thrust the lamp into her hand, turned and disappeared in the gloom. Shivering, Lucy hurried to the room at the end of the corridor.

It was dank and cold and musty smelling, like the inside of a trunk that has been in a cellar for years. The bed was an old brass four-poster with an ancient looking patchwork quilt on it. Alongside the door to the room was another door covered by a full-length mirror in a cracked gilt frame.

As she closed the hall door, a sudden thunderclap shook the earth, making the whole room tremble. It so startled Lucy that a little cry of terror escaped from her lips. "Now stop that!" she said to herself aloud. "You're just being silly, Lucy Carter!"

The sound of her voice was reassuring, and she set about getting ready for bed. As she opened her overnight bag and took out the few things she needed, the light from the kerosene lamp dimmed and a flash of lightning burst across the sky. Seconds later came a thunderclap so loud that she jumped in fright. There was a sudden draft of icy air in the room and Lucy whirled in its direction.

"Oh!" she gasped, for there standing beyond the foot of the bed was the shadowy figure of a dark-haired woman. Lamplight seemed to glow in her eyes, and she wore a long, flowing gown of moldy green velvet. She stood there without speaking, and the silence grew. After Lucy's first fright, she decided this must be the same woman who had told the old man to let her stay for the night. So she said, "Thank you for speaking up for me before. I really didn't want to drive farther in this weather."

But the woman didn't answer. She simply stared at Lucy with those strangely lighted eyes, then shook her head slowly, and turned to leave the room. Moving with a gliding motion she headed toward the door — but not the one that led to the hallway. Lucy was just about to speak when the woman *walked right into the mirror and vanished!*

Heart pounding with terror, Lucy stood frozen to the spot, too frightened even to cry out. *The woman in the green velvet dress had cast no reflection in the mirror!* She must have been a ghost. Lucy had just talked with a ghost!

Just as the dim lamplight burned out, another flash of lightning zigzagged across the sky sending a bluish glare into the room. It was followed almost instantly by a heavy clap of thunder. Before it had rumbled off into the distance Lucy had jumped into bed and pulled the musty covers over her head. She lay there tense and shivering. Though locked doors couldn't keep ghosts away, at least huddled under the quilt she could keep from seeing them.

For a long while Lucy lay there, terrified. The storm had moved on after that last terrible bolt of lightning. Now the rumblings, the slashing rain, and the wailing of the wind slowly faded and finally Lucy slept.

When she awakened it was morning. Sunlight streamed in through the cobwebbed window. But the room had changed from dinginess to ruin. The glass in the window was broken and the curtains hung in wispy shreds. As she jumped out of bed, a cloud of dust arose from the filthy covers. The dank and musty smell was stronger than ever, and the bare floor was dust-covered except for her footprints. Then Lucy looked toward the door with the mirror. The wooden frame flecked with gilt sagged — and the glass was gone.

Now, in the bright light of morning, Lucy felt she had to know what was behind that door. She knew that ghosts often haunt the scene of violent death. What had the ghost of the woman in the green gown been trying to reveal?

She hesitated a moment then impulsively went to the door, grasped the knob, and tried to turn it. It seemed to be stuck. But now she was really determined to find out what lay behind it. Grasping the knob with both hands and twisting it as hard as she could, she pulled and tugged with all her strength.

Finally the door yielded. It swung open, creaking loudly as the long, unused hinges rubbed against one another. A cloud of dust arose and with it a sickening smell of decay. Lucy, dreading what her eyes might see in the dark gloom, gasped. She staggered back.

There, huddled in the corner of the closet, was a grinning skeleton surrounded by tatters of rotting green velvet!

Lucy hurriedly gathered her belongings, and seizing her handbag, dashed from the room. She fled down the dusty corridor to the lobby — and could hardly believe her eyes! The place looked deserted and as if it had been abandoned for years. The few pieces of furniture were rotting and falling apart. Dark cobwebs filled all the corners, and dust, thick gray dust, lay like a soft cover over everything. But most frightening — there was only *one* set of footprints in the dust. *Her own!*

Panic rising in her throat, Lucy pushed open the heavy, creaking front door and ran to her car. As the motor roared into life, she took one last look at the Old Graystone Inn. Once again shudders of horror went down her spine. The entire front of the place was completely *boarded up!* Even the front door was boarded tight. How had she been able to leave? *Had she really spent that awful night there?*

Lucy sped away from the ghastly place. "But I *did* see lights there," she said aloud. "And there *was* the old couple who let me in. Who were they?"

Perhaps they were spirits sent to help travelers like Lucy, caught in a terrible storm at night. Perhaps — ghostly murderers.

Lucy Carter would never know.

The Phantom's Gold

In a little Welsh town with the unpronounceable name of Ystradgynlais, there once lived a man named Tom Llewellyn.

Tom was walking home late one evening along a dark and lonely lane when he came face-to-face with the strangely-clad ghost of a beautiful woman. On her head was tied a scarf marked with a skull and crossbones. From her ears dangled golden hoops, and below her flowing cape, Tom could see she wore heavy pirate-fashion boots. A weird bluish light glowed around her and her face was pale, her eyes deep-set and sad. Looming up there in the middle of the path, arms outspread as if she were trying to bar his way, she nearly frightened poor Tom out of his wits. He froze in his tracks, then summoning all his courage, he ran past her. He kept running as fast as he could for home and safety.

Tom made up his mind never to walk along that lane after dark. But the next night he met her again — this time in an entirely different place. Just as before, there was the bluish glow, the pale white face, and the deep-set sad eyes. Again, Tom managed to escape her, but he didn't sleep very well that night. He tossed and turned, fearing to fall asleep lest he have nightmares.

For weeks he kept meeting the ghost and running from her. Finally he made up his mind he must ask why she was haunting him.

"Do not be afraid of me, Thomas Llewellyn," she said in a hollow, eerie voice. "I will not hurt you. But you must promise to do me a service or I will haunt you forever."

Not wanting to be haunted for even another night, he asked her what it was she wanted him to do, and she told him. Strange as it seemed, the ghost wanted Tom to go across the Atlantic Ocean — to a certain house in Charleston, South Carolina. There he was to remove a box from its hiding place.

Tom was thunderstruck. "I am a poor man," he explained. "I couldn't afford to make a trip all the way to America!"

But the ghost remained steadfast. "Meet me next Friday night when the clock strikes twelve," she ordered, "at the gate to the village graveyard!" And with that she vanished.

Tom could hardly wait to tell his friends what had happened. One of them happened to be the pastor of the village parish and he immediately called a prayer meeting for the following Friday night in hopes of making the ghost go away. But when the meeting was over and everyone was leaving the church, there was suddenly a strange rushing of wind and Tom Llewellyn disappeared from sight. There was great consternation among the villagers, and after searching for hours, they all went sadly home.

To everyone's amazement Tom turned up the next morning with the strangest tale they had ever heard. "I was snatched into the air, taken to the river and dumped in the water," he said. "Then when I picked myself up and climbed out, who should I see but the ghost. She was in a fair fury, she was! Her eyes sparkled like coals and she shook her finger at me, and gave me a tongue lashing like I never heard before. She said she was angry because I had told you about her and didn't show up on the dot of midnight. But she calmed down and promised not to hurt me. Then all of a sudden I felt myself being lifted into the air and whisked away with the swiftness of the wind."

He paused a moment, then said, "Finally, after what seemed a long time, I was put on the ground before an empty dark house. Before I could turn around, there was the ghost beside me and she told me to follow her inside. Well, we went into the house and it was fearful dark. I could hear the flapping of bats' wings, the pitter patter of rats scurrying about behind walls. And I could feel the tickle of spiderwebs hitting me in the face. Oh, I was scared, you can be sure of that. If it hadn't been for the pale blue glow of the ghost I couldn't have seen a thing. It was a terrible house. It smelled dank and musty. The floorboards creaked, and I almost fell down the stairs to the cellar. The ghost finally took me to a tiny room and made me lift up a floorboard in the corner. And there was the box."

The villagers listened, spellbound, as Tom told them the rest of his strange story. "I stood there alone with that ghost, and she pointed to the box and said, 'Take it up, Thomas, and open it.'

"I did. And it was full of gold coins! Then she nodded and said, 'Very well. Now you must take the box three miles to the east and cast it into the ocean.'"

"And then what?" asked the villagers impatiently.

"I closed the box and tucked it under my arm," Tom said. "Then I felt myself lifted in the air again, carried through an open window, and away into the darkness of the night. I was put down — quite gently — at the edge of the huge black ocean."

"'Cast the box into the sea!' the ghost commanded me.

"I flung it as hard as I could, and when it hit the water there was an ear-splitting roar like a thousand thunderclaps! Next, I was whisked into the air again. After a time I was put back on the ground outside the church right here in Ystradgynlais. There she was — right beside me, nodding her head."

Once again Tom paused.

"What happened then?" his friends asked.

Tom continued. " 'You have done well, Thomas,' she said to me. 'I will now tell you a secret, which you must never reveal to a living soul. Then I shall leave you never to return again.'

"She leaned over and whispered in my ear. She was so close I could feel her icy breath. Then she backed away, raised her right arm and said, 'Farewell, Thomas.' "

"And then what?" Tom's friends gasped.

"Then she vanished," he replied.

"But what did she *tell* you?" the villagers asked.

Tom shook his head. "I'll not break my word. I shall never tell a living soul."

Of course, everyone in the village tried to guess what it was that the ghost had told Tom, but he never would say anything more about it. But one old man recalled that Tom's description of the ghost fitted a certain Elizabeth Gething, who long ago had left the village and gone off to live in Charleston, South Carolina, where she became a lady pirate.

"I was just a little lad at the time," the old man told the villagers. "But I remember hearing folks talk about her. They said she was as fierce as Blackbeard and Captain Kidd. Many a good man was sent to Davy Jones' Locker by that woman, and all for the sake of gold!" The old man sighed, shook his head and went on. "Final justice, that's what it was. Her spirit couldn't rest until she gave back to the sea what she had stolen from it."

Riding a Tombstone

LATE ONE very dark night, a man traveling along a lonely country road on his way home from a party, saw a figure coming toward him. To his amazement he saw that it was an old friend of his — but an old friend *who had been dead for ten years!* He was even more surprised when the dead man smiled and said, "How are you, old friend? I hope you are feeling well."

"I couldn't be feeling better," answered the traveler, by now so astonished that he even forgot the fact that his friend *was* dead. "How about you?"

"I'm just fine," said the dead man, "so

fine, in fact, I think you should come to my house so that we may drink to each other's health."

"That's a wonderful idea," agreed the traveler. "I couldn't have come up with a better suggestion myself for such a happy occasion."

So arm in arm they went off until they came to a house where they entered, sat down and talked for hours. Eventually the traveler began to yawn. "Shiver my liver!" he said. "It's nearly daybreak. I must be off."

"Oh, stay a while longer," urged the dead man. "Why go so early? You can sleep here if you wish."

"No, my friend," said the other. "I simply can't stay. I've too much business to attend to, and as it is I'll sleep away half the day."

"Well, if you must go then, I won't keep you. But there's no sense in your walking. Get on my horse, it will carry you home quickly and in safety."

"That's very kind of you, old friend. Thank you."

And with that the traveler climbed on the horse which began galloping off with the speed of a whirlwind. Suddenly he heard a cock crow in the distance, then the earth began to tremble, the wind began to blow, and thunderclaps rumbled across the heavens. Frightened out of his wits the man hung on for dear life. Suddenly, the rosy fingers of dawn began lighting the sky, and he could see the countryside through which he passed. It was awful! All around were graves and tombstones. And beneath him, not a galloping horse, but the biggest, coldest tombstone of them all!

The Headless Princess

LONG AGO, in a kingdom that no longer exists, lived a princess who was a sorceress. Not far from the royal palace an old priest dwelt in a small cottage. He had living with him a nephew who had been left an orphan when he was an infant. The boy was ten years old and very quick and alert. Every day he went to the house of a wise old woman who taught him many things.

Now it happened that one day as he came home from his lessons late in the evening, he passed the palace and looked in one of the windows. There sat the princess before a mirror. As he watched, he was amazed to see her take off her head! She proceeded to lather it with soap and wash it with clean water. Then she combed the hair, and pleated it in a long black braid. Finally, she put the combed and laundered head back in its proper place on her neck.

The boy couldn't believe his eyes! "She must be a witch!" he gasped.

When he got home he told his uncle, and everyone who came to visit, how he had seen the princess without her head. Some scoffed, but many believed him.

Not long after this the princess became seriously ill, and she sent for her father the king, saying, "If I die, make the priest's nephew read psalms over me for three nights in a row."

The king agreed to carry out her last wish, and in a few days she died. The king had her body placed in a richly carved, heavy oak coffin and carried to the church. Then the king summoned the priest, and asked, "Have you a nephew?"

"I have, Your Majesty."

"Well then, I command that he read psalms over my daughter for three nights in a row."

"So be it, Your Majesty," replied the old

priest, and with that he returned to his cottage.

In the morning the priest told his nephew to get ready to carry out the king's command that night. The boy quickly gathered up his books and went to the old woman's house to do his daily lessons, but he looked so gloomy that she said to him, "What are you so unhappy about?"

"How can I help being unhappy," he replied. "Something terrible is going to happen to me tonight."

"What do you mean by that? Speak up now, and tell me the truth."

"Well, granny, if you must know, I've got to go and read psalms over the dead princess. But I know she was a witch and I'm afraid."

"I knew she was a witch long before you did," said the old woman. "But never you mind. If you do exactly as I tell you there will be nothing to fear. Here, take this knife. . . . Good. Now, when you go into the church tonight, trace a circle around yourself with the point of the knife, then read from your book of psalms. Whatever you do, don't look behind you! Whatever happens, whatever horrors appear, do not look up but go on reading. If you look behind you even once, it will be the end of you."

That evening the boy went to church and traced a circle around him with the knife, just as the old woman had instructed him. Then he opened his book of psalms and began to read. It was dark and lonely. There were creaking sounds from time to time, and the chill night air sent shivers down his back. But he stood there reading and not looking once behind him.

Then the clock began striking midnight . . . and at the last two strokes . . . Bong! Bong! The heavy lid of the coffin began to creak. Slowly it opened, then, when it was halfway up it flew all the way with a bang! The princess leaped out, her eyes gleaming ferociously, her face pale, and her nails like claws of a wild beast.

"Now I'll teach you to go peeping through my windows, and telling the world what you saw!" she snarled.

She rushed at him but when she got to the edge of the circle it was as if she had bumped into an invisible wall — as if he were surrounded by unbreakable glass. The princess howled and shrieked and gnashed her teeth, she roared and moaned and stamped her feet, but she could not get at the boy. Trembling as he read, the boy did exactly as he had been told. He stood in his protected circle reading aloud, not daring to look anywhere but at the pages of his book. Finally daybreak came and the princess hurried back to her coffin and pulled down the lid with a crash.

The next night everything happened in exactly the same way as on the first night, but the priest's nephew was not as afraid, because he felt he was safe. He kept reading until dawn, and in the morning he went to the old woman for his lessons, as usual. She asked him, "Well, have you seen any horrors?"

"Yes, granny," he said.

"It will be even worse tonight," she declared. "But do as I have told you, and no harm will come."

That evening the boy went back to the church and drew the circle with the knife as he had before. Then he began to read, with a fast-beating heart. Tonight he was frightened because the woman had told him the princess would try something worse.

At the last two strokes of midnight the heavy coffin lid began to creak open as before. Slowly at first . . . creak! . . . creak! It fell back, and as it did a thunderclap echoed through the church. The princess leaped out, shrieking such terrible curses that the boy quaked with terror. The creature flung herself at him, only to be stopped at the edge of the circle as she had before. But this time she backed away, raised her arms and began muttering in a fearful chant. Now wails and moans began filling the air. Bats flew in the windows. The very walls burst open, and grinning skeletons, with blue flames shooting from their skulls, came dancing out. The boy's heart pounded with terror, but he stood his ground and kept reading.

Then suddenly the earth seemed to tremble. A low rumbling noise was heard and, horror of horrors! The walls of the church burst into brilliant orange flames that cracked and roared and licked at his feet. He felt the intense heat and smelled a hot sulphurous odor. He was nearly fainting but he looked neither to the right nor to the left, nor in front nor behind him, but directly into his book of psalms.

Finally the first light of dawn began to appear behind the stained glass windows. The princess uttered one last horrible scream, then rushed back to her coffin, flung herself into it, and pulled down the heavy lid. The minute the lid banged shut, the flames disappeared and the skeletons and bats vanished. All was still and peaceful.

But then a strange thing happened. The heavy lid suddenly flew off the coffin and crashed down to the floor. For a moment the boy stood motionless, but all remained silent. As the morning sun came streaming in, he no longer felt afraid.

The boy was just getting ready to leave when the church door opened and in came the king. He saw that the coffin in which his daughter lay was open. Then he noticed that she was lying face down. He frowned at the boy and said sternly, "What is the meaning of this?"

When the boy told him what had happened, the king turned pale — for he already knew in his heart that his daughter was a witch. He had heard stories, now he had to believe them. His daughter lay as witches lie — face down. And no ten-year-old boy could have lifted the heavy coffin lid.

So calling his servants, the king ordered that his daughter's body be burned to ashes so that the witch's ghost could do no further harm.

Then summoning the boy to him, he said, "You are a brave lad, for you have dared to defy a witch. And for that you shall be rewarded with enough gold to keep you for the rest of your life."

And being a wise boy, as well as a brave one, he in turn rewarded his uncle, the priest, and the old woman who had helped him to outwit the witch. So instead of one person, all three lived in comfort for the rest of their lives.

The Woman Who Climbed
from Her Grave

Some years ago, a woman died in a little town in Austria. Her name was Mrs. Zeller. An aging widow who lived with her daughter and family, Mrs. Zeller had passed away rather suddenly, and after the usual mourning period her body was buried in the village churchyard. The funeral itself was very elaborate and took place with great ceremony for she had been an important woman in town. Her family arrayed her in her finest clothes and placed on one of her fingers a beautiful diamond ring she had prized very highly during her life.

That night after the funeral, one of the

undertaker's men, having noticed the ring, made up his mind to rob the grave. After midnight, when it was dark and quiet, he took the necessary tools, sneaked into the cemetery, and began digging up the newly made grave by the light of a dim hooded lantern. When he finally struck the coffin he removed the lid at once. Suddenly the "corpse" began to stir. Wild with terror, the would-be thief fled from the grave as its moaning occupant sat up stiffly and began to climb painfully out of the grave.

Little did the man know that the terrible crime he had planned, of robbing the dead, would be a blessing in disguise. For Mrs. Zeller had fallen into a deathlike trance and had been mistakenly buried alive. Alone in the dark, the poor woman managed to pull herself up to the surface of the ground. Then she walked all the way home in her shroud, and rang the front doorbell of her house! You can imagine how horrified her family must have felt when they opened the door and saw her standing there!

Fortunately, they realized what had happened, and did not think they were being haunted. Mrs. Zeller recovered and lived for many years after her escape from her grave.

The Banshee Whose Feelings
Were Hurt

THERE ARE very few Irishmen, anywhere
in the world, who have the slightest doubt
about the existence of banshees, for even if
they don't have one in their own family, they
always know someone who has.

Now, a banshee sometimes appears as a
beautiful maiden; at other times, as a hideous
old hag, withered and bent, clad in a shroud
of deepest black. She only appears to members of a family on the eve of a death, at
which time she takes her stand outside the
house to wail and cry and shriek and moan,
until all within are awakened. She goes on
howling and mourning until the object of her

visit is no more. With that she departs and does not return again until a similar sad occasion demands her presence.

It is said about banshees that they are easily insulted and, if so, will angrily leave. Then they shun the family until the last member of that generation has died. This is the story of just such a banshee.

John Dooley, a well-to-do farmer, was one man who did scoff at the very notion of a banshee. He was a gloomy man who had few friends, but no enemies either. His home was taken care of by his old housekeeper, Moya. Moya loved to tell wild and hair-raising tales about ghosts and goblins and wolf-men and fairies. Luckily she enjoyed her own stories, for John Dooley did not. But no matter how he scoffed and made fun of her, she did not change her opinions.

One morning Moya came to Dooley in a terrible state of nerves. "Och," she said, "I'm afraid that there's trouble and misfortune hangin' over us."

"And what makes you think so?" John asked with a half smile.

"Och!" she replied, "I'm heart-scalded to tell you, and know you'll laugh at me, but there's something bad over us. A banshee was about the house all night. She has me all frightened out of me wits with her shoutin' and bawlin'."

"And what did she look like?" John Dooley asked. "I suppose you can tell me?"

"Indeed I can," Moya said. "I saw her at the little window over me bed; a kind of reddish light shone around the house. I looked up, and there I saw her old, pale face, and glassy eyes lookin' in as she rocked to and fro, clapping her little withered hands, and cryin' as if her heart would break."

John shrugged, "You saw no more than trick of moonlight and shadow," he said. "Now forget such foolishness and make my breakfast. I must go into town this day and I want to return before dark."

But instead of obeying him, Moya stood there trembling. Tears streamed down her wrinkled cheeks. "For heaven's sake, Master John, don't go today," she begged. "Wait till some other day, and God bless you, for if you go today something evil will happen."

John Dooley paid no attention to her pleas and again told her to put breakfast on the table. This time she did as she was told, weeping the whole time.

But even as he bundled himself up against the brisk November winds she tried to prevent him from leaving the house. "Don't go today!" she begged. "I know more of these things than you do, and I tell you that if you leave you'll never come through this door again with your life."

But away John Dooley went. After all, he was a man afraid of nothing.

His business in town finished, John unexpectedly met an old friend he had not seen in years, so they agreed to dine together. They fell to talking and before either of them realized it the moon had risen. It was late at night when John finally mounted his horse for the long and lonely ride home.

At the farm poor old Moya had become more and more worried as night came on and John Dooley still had not returned. Finally when she heard the sound of hoofbeats pounding up the lane, she ran out into the dark and windy night. There was John Dooley's riderless horse — smeared with blood!

As quickly as possible she raised the alarm, and a party of men volunteered to go out and search for their missing neighbor. Before dawn they found his body lying in a ditch. Evidently he had been robbed and killed by highwaymen.

John Dooley was buried in the local churchyard. His property was left to a brother who lived in London, but until he could come to claim it, two neighbors were appointed to guard the house.

They had been the dead man's closest friends — Jack O'Malley and Harry Taylor. Jack was a huge man who feared no *living* creature, but who was so respectful of the dead that he was known to travel miles out of his way to avoid a haunt. Harry, like John Dooley, scorned such things as ghosts, goblins, leprechauns and elves. But in spite of their differences of opinion, the two men were fast friends.

It was the sixth or seventh night of their lonely vigil. Hector, Jack's huge mastiff, dozed before the cheerful turf fire that blazed on the hearth, and old Moya slept soundly in the chimney corner on a straw pallet. The two friends sat at a small oak table and as they talked fondly of good times past, Jack spoke of the banshee and said that he hoped she would not come to disturb their watch.

"Devil take the banshee!" exclaimed Harry. "You're too superstitious for your own good. I'd like to see the face of anything dead or alive that would dare appear here!" Seizing a pistol from the table and glancing sternly at his friend he added, "By Heaven, I'd empty this into any banshee who dared come here tonight!"

Jack turned pale. "Better for you to shoot the sheriff than to fire at the banshee."

"Bah!" roared Harry. "You and your banshee!"

Their talk continued until the wee hours of the night when both men became drowsy. They blew out the candle, rested their heads on the table, and caught a few winks of sleep. Soon there was no sound in the room but the ticking of the clock and the snoring of old Moya in the chimney corner.

Neither knew how long they had been sleeping, when they were awakened by a wild and blood curdling shriek. It was Moya. "Oh, the banshee!" she screamed. "The banshee! Lord have mercy on us, she's back again and I've never heard her so wild in all me days!"

Jack O'Malley turned pale, for he believed every word she said. Harry Taylor, on the other hand decided there must be someone skulking about outside. Each man for his own reasons listened carefully, but heard nothing. Nevertheless, they went out to search the grounds. They found nothing. Returning to the kitchen they decided to drink the tea that Moya brewed for them.

A few moments later there was an unearthly howl. Even Harry agreed that it was enough to wake the dead.

"The banshee again!" cried Moya.

Jack's knees turned to jelly. Harry jumped up and seized his weapon.

"No, no Harry, don't go out," said Jack. "There's nothing for us to fear in here."

Keeping a firm grip on the weapon, Harry sat down again. Meanwhile Moya dropped to her knees and began praying and wailing. There was *something* outside, and only Harry had any doubts as to what it was.

Again the mournful cry pierced the air, only now it was louder and wilder than before. Now it came from the window, now from the door. At times it issued from the chimney, and even from the very floor beneath their feet. It rose to a fearsome yell that seemed to burst from a thousand throats. It rose and fell like a sobbing wind. It wailed and howled like an angry demon. And for nearly a quarter of an hour the terrible voice continued to shatter the silence. Then came the heavy creaking sound of a large wagon and the thud and crunch of horses' hoofs. Then there was the sound of a powerful rushing wind.

Around and around the house the sounds went — once, twice, three times, then silence. Jack and Moya were pale as ghosts. Even Harry was trembling.

"It's the death coach," murmured Moya. "I've often heard it and seen it before."

"You've actually seen it?" asked Harry. "Tell us what it's like."

"Why," she answered, her voice hoarse with terror, "it's like any other coach, but twice as big and hung over with black cloth and a black coffin on the top of it. And it's drawn by headless horses."

"Heaven help us!" Jack exclaimed.

"Maybe it's the banshee coming for Moya," declared Harry, grinning and winking at Jack.

"No, no!" she exclaimed. "I'm not one of the family. *It comes for John Dooley's brother yet to arrive from England!*"

Suddenly the dreadful shrieking and the awful clatter began again.

"Open the door, Jack," ordered Harry. "Put Hector out! He'll scare off whoever it is."

But when his master opened the door the dog refused to go out. His hair stood up and he trembled like a leaf, howling mournfully all the while.

"You cowardly beast!" shouted Harry.

He pushed the dog out into the darkness. The mastiff, with a final hideous howl, fell to the ground and lay still as if struck by a great invisible club.

"That does it," said Harry, grabbing his weapon. "Follow me, Jack, and don't forget your pistols. I'll have a crack at this infernal demon or die trying."

"I'll follow you to the death," answered Jack, "but I wouldn't fire at the banshee for all the leprechauns' gold."

It was Harry who first caught sight of the ghastly banshee. He pulled the trigger of his pistol and blasted away in a thunderous explosion that shattered the night. An ear splitting scream followed ten times louder and more horrible than they had heard before. The hair rose up on their heads and cold sweat ran down their faces. A terrible reddish-blue light shone round the house and the death coach came into view. It was drawn by six headless black horses. Then the figure of a withered old hag, surrounded by blue flame came running across the yard. She climbed into the carriage and drove off with a dreadful clatter. As the coach passed, the old hag cast her burning eyes on the two men, scowling fiercely as she shook her bony fist at them. And even after they were gone from sight the clatter of the wheels, the thunder of horses' hoofs, and the appalling shrieks of the banshee could still be heard.

When John's brother arrived from England he was told of the awful experience of that terrible night, and he dreaded the return of the banshee. But as long as one member of that generation of Dooleys lived, the banshee never returned.

The Family Banshee had been insulted!

The Ghost Who Helped a Ghost

LONG AGO in China a man named Ku
went to a Buddhist temple one night and
asked the chief priest if he might sleep
there, for it was too late for him to travel
the necessary distance to his home.

"Very well," said the priest. "You are
welcome to lodge here for the night. I am
going with my disciples to say prayers over
a dead man who is being placed in his
coffin tonight."

Ku thanked the priest, and as soon as he
was alone he closed the door, put out the

lamp, lay down, and in a few minutes he was asleep.

But at midnight he was awakened by a loud knocking at the door. "Who is there?" asked Ku.

"It is your old friend, Shen Ting-Lan," replied the voice from outside. It so happened that Ku's friend, Shen, had died ten years earlier, so Ku became terribly frightened.

"Don't be afraid," came the voice. "I wish you no harm. I merely desire to tell you something of great importance. Had I wanted to harm you I would have come in uninvited, as I am a ghost and can do such things. I knocked so that I wouldn't frighten you by appearing too suddenly."

This sounded reasonable to Ku, so he opened the door. He saw instantly that the figure standing there was not Shen. It entered, but after taking only a few steps, fell flat on the floor. Ku rushed off to light the lamp.

"Wait!" called the voice, which now came from the motionless figure lying on the floor. "Hear me first. I am the man who is being put in the coffin tonight. My faithless wife poisoned me. The ghost of Shen Ting-Lan sent me to you for help and I look to you for justice."

"But I am not a magistrate," replied Ku. "How can I obtain justice for you?"

"Ask for a hearing on the cause of my death. That will prove the truth of my words. You may get a lamp now. But when the light shines upon me I shall be able to speak no more. That will not be important, for I have nothing more to reveal."

Just then there was another knock on the door and Ku called out, "Who is it?"

It was the chief priest of the temple with his followers. "While we were reciting the appropriate prayers as the body was being carried to the coffin, it vanished," he said excitedly. "Have you heard any strange noises here? The body must be *some* place!"

"It is here," said Ku. Hastily, he lighted the lamp and they all bent down to examine the body on the floor.

"This man has been poisoned!" the chief priest said. "He has not died a natural death."

Quickly, Ku told his strange story. The chief priest nodded. "We shall go to the magistrate in the morning," he said. "He must be told of this."

And so it was that a guilty person was brought to justice — and all because a *ghost helped a ghost.*

The Poltergeist with
the Heart of a Genie

GEORGE AND LINDA RICH were looking forward to vacationing at the new beach house
they had taken for the summer — lots of
sunshine, picnics by the sea, and fun-filled
visits from their friends in the city.

The main reason they had chosen this
particular beach house was because of the
piano which was part of the furnishings.
George happened to be an accomplished
pianist and Linda had a very good voice.
So when the weather was bad, or they didn't
feel like going to the beach they would
enjoy singing and playing. They would
never have to worry about what to do.

And when friends came over it would be a way of entertaining them.

The weather wasn't very promising the day that they first moved in. The sky was gray and the wind made the beach an uncomfortable place to be. This didn't bother George and Linda because they were busy getting the place in order. It was not until well after midnight that they were finally ready for bed.

"I'm exhausted!" exclaimed George. "I'll bet I could sleep the clock around."

"Me too," agreed Linda. "But I'll bet we both wake up with the sun tomorrow."

"Well, I hope this weather changes and we'll see the sun, tomorrow," answered George.

They both slept soundly until the middle of the night when they were awakened by a terrible crash. It sounded as if a truck had emptied a load of bricks on the roof.

"Good heavens! What's that?" gasped Linda, sitting bolt upright.

"The roof!" George cried. "I'd better go see what's wrong."

"Be careful!" cautioned Linda. "Maybe the chimney has fallen in."

"I don't think so," he replied. "You stay here. I'll be right back."

By now the noise was so loud that they had to shout in order to hear one another. They turned on the lights, George slipped on his bathrobe, snatched up a flashlight, and ran to the front door. But the very instant that his hand touched the doorknob the noise stopped. There was dead silence, in fact. Only the gentle murmur of the waves along the beach could be heard. George opened the door, and flashed the light beam around outside.

"Well I'll be . . . !" he proclaimed, his eyes widening. He could hardly believe what he saw. There, all around the house, glittering and gleaming with every color of the rainbow, were thousands and thousands of marbles, just like the ones he used to play with when he was a boy. There were big ones and little ones, reds and greens and yellows, milkies and blooddies, and aggies. It was as if every marble in the world had suddenly dropped out of the sky and bounced off his beach house roof. It was like a dream, yet he knew he wasn't dreaming. Bending down and picking up a beautiful red, white, and blue shooter, he looked at it, and put it in his bathrobe pocket.

"Wait till Linda sees this," he thought, and hurried back upstairs.

Linda was amazed! "I'm going down to see for myself," she said.

After only a few minutes she was back in the bedroom — and she looked furious.

"George Rich!" she exclaimed. "You ought to be ashamed of yourself, fibbing like that."

"What do you mean?" he demanded, a look of surprise on his face.

"All that talk about marbles! Really now! I saw for myself. If you can call this a marble, then you'd better go out and have your eyes examined!" And with that she held out her hand, and in it was a lump of coal.

"But you *saw* the marble," George exclaimed. "Here, look!" He reached into his bathrobe pocket — and drew out *another chunk of coal!*

The next morning when they looked outside they were even more amazed than they had been the night before. Not only were there no marbles, there was no coal either. It was as if nothing at all had happened during the night. After searching everywhere and finding nothing, George and Linda finally went back to getting the beach house in order. Nothing happened for the rest of the day, or that evening, either. Just before bedtime they decided to try out the piano, so they sat down together and played and sang for about an hour.

There were no noises at all that night, so they slept soundly till morning.

The surprise came before breakfast. The top of the piano was covered with flowers. The dining table was set with crystal goblets, golden knives, forks, and spoons, silver cups, and dishes of the finest bone china. Not only that, but there were platters heaped with freshly scrambled eggs, crisp bacon, piping hot biscuits dripping with fresh butter, oranges, steaming coffee, and five different kinds of jelly and jam. They could hardly believe their eyes. Then Linda noticed something covered up by a gleaming white napkin. "I wonder what's under that?" she asked, in wide-eyed astonishment.

"There's only one way to find out," replied George, and he pulled away the napkin.

"Ohhh!" exclaimed Linda. "It can't be! It just can't be!"

George blinked, rubbed his eyes and looked again. "But it is! See?" He reached out and touched the object that had been under the napkin — a crystal ice bucket filled to the brim with shiny, new silver dollars!

It was all they could do to contain their excitement and sit down to the fabulous breakfast that had been so mysteriously spread out for them. "The only thing I can think of," said Linda jokingly, "is that we've a poltergeist in this house that likes us."

At which point, as if in reply to what she had said, there was an outburst of high pitched, tinkling laughter. Then, before either one of them could say another word, the bucket of coins rose slowly up in the air before their eyes. Sailing straight across the room it stopped near the window, turned upside down, and sent a shower of silver tumbling over the floor, and the voice laughed delightedly.

Now too excited to do more than nibble at the breakfast, George and Linda were next nearly frightened out of their wits when every single thing on the table suddenly flew together with a mighty crash, then vanished from sight. Only the overturned bucket and the scattered silver dollars remained.

Needless to say, from that day on, life in the beach house was never the same again. With all those silver dollars — three hundred and ninety-two to be exact, they went out for dinner that night, feeling rich in money as well as in name. They came home very late and went straight to bed.

But unfortunately there was no sleep for them. Their heads had barely touched the pillows when the beds began to shake. The room shook and trembled, the windows rattled, and objects began flying through the air, crashing against the walls and falling to the floor. Angry shrieks rang out downstairs, and a sound of angry banging on the piano keys could be heard.

George, worried that whatever it was causing the disturbance might damage the piano, jumped out of bed, ran down to the living room and turned on the light. The moment he reached the piano all the clamor stopped and the house became silent. "I wonder if it's angry because I didn't play for it tonight?" he asked himself. And with that he sat down and began to play.

"George!" called Linda from the bedroom. "Why on earth are you playing the piano?"

"Just a minute," he called back. "I'll explain." He kept on playing, and as he did so, he looked around. Though he saw nobody, he said, "Now listen, whoever you are . . . or *whatever* you may be. . . . We don't mean you any harm, and I think you don't mean us harm either. That was a great breakfast this morning. And those silver dollars . . . fantastic! But we have to get some rest at night. So, suppose we make a bargain. If you'll promise not to make noises at night, or do anything else to wake us up or scare us, I'll play the piano for you every night before I go to bed. Is that a deal? And I'll tell you something else, you won't even have to make breakfast for us, or do anything else either."

At that he heard a peal of laughter, just like the laughter he and Linda had heard at breakfast. He wasn't sure whether it meant "Yes," or "No," but to be on the safe side he played a lullaby. Then getting up, he looked around the room and said softly, "Good night, friend."

This time, instead of hearing a laugh, George was certain he could hear what sounded like a gentle little giggle. He smiled to himself, turned out the light, and went back to the bedroom.

There were no more disturbances for the rest of the night, and at breakfast in the morning there was another table full of food and beautiful objects. There were also flowers all over the house. Most exciting of all were the contents of the little boxes George and Linda found alongside their plates — a string of pearls for her and a waterproof wristwatch for him.

"Nobody would ever believe us," said George, shaking his head.

"Who cares?" answered Linda smiling.

So they made up their minds to say nothing to anyone, and for the rest of their summer at the beach they had a marvelous time. Every night they played some music for their poltergeist, and every day it did something nice for them in the way of a present or a favor. The poltergeist even helped George and Linda entertain their friends when they had parties. By making things appear and disappear at the right times, it made everyone think that George was an accomplished magician.

When the summer was finally over and it was time to go back to the city for good, they were just as sorry to leave their friendly poltergeist as they were that vacation had ended.

"You know," said Linda, as they were driving away from the beach house for the last time, "when you think of all the lovely presents our friend gave us, I wonder — was it a poltergeist? Or was it a genie?"

George smiled. "I can't say for sure," he said, "but if you ask me our friend was *a poltergeist with the heart of a genie!*"